MAR 1 3

For Juliet, with love —S.L.J.

For Señor Leal y Señor Lowe, besos —S.H.

Text copyright © 2011 by Sally Lloyd-Jones ﺱ Cover art and interior illustrations copyright © 2011 by Sue Heap ﺱ All rights reserved. Published in the United States by Schwartz & Wade Books, an imprint of Random House Children's Books, a division of Random House, Inc., New York. ﺱ Schwartz & Wade Books and the colophon are trademarks of Random House, Inc.

Visit us on the Web! www.randomhouse.com/kids ﺱ Educators and librarians, for a variety of teaching tools, visit us at www.randomhouse.com/teachers

Library of Congress Cataloging-in-Publication Data
Lloyd-Jones, Sally. ﺱ How to get a job—by me, the boss / and Sally Lloyd-Jones and Sue Heap.— 1st ed. ﺱ p. cm. ﺱ Summary: A young girl describes in detail how to decide on an interesting job and then tells exactly how to go about getting it. ﺱ ISBN 978-0-375-86664-7 (trade) — ISBN 978-0-375-96664-4 (glb) ﺱ [1. Occupations—Fiction.] I. Heap, Sue. II. Title. ﺱ PZ7.L77878Ho 2011 [E]—dc22 ﺱ 2009050696

The text of this book is set in Stempel Garamond. ﺱ The illustrations were rendered in acrylic paint, crayons, and a 0.7-millimeter felt-tip pen. ﺱ Book design by Rachael Cole

MANUFACTURED IN CHINA
10 9 8 7 6 5 4 3 2 1
First Edition

How to get a JOB by Me, The Boss

and Sally Lloyd-Jones
and Sue Heap

MY CHAIR

schwartz & wade books · new york

If you want to get a Job, first you need to know what exactly a Job is.

A Job is so you can have something to do
and get money for your family.

And sometimes a Job is so you can
get all dressed up and wear
your new shoes to work.

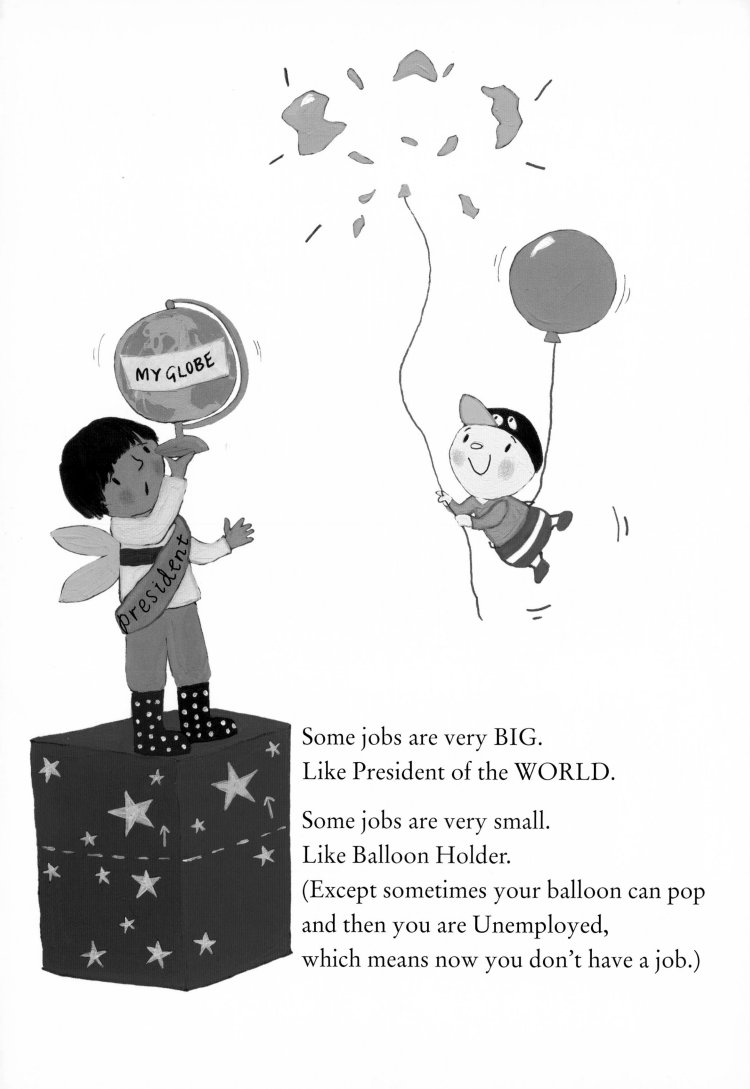

Some jobs are very BIG.
Like President of the WORLD.

Some jobs are very small.
Like Balloon Holder.
(Except sometimes your balloon can pop
and then you are Unemployed,
which means now you don't have a job.)

HERE'S WHAT ISN'T A JOB:
★ Sitting in your chair eating cookies
(School is a sort of job because you do HOMEWORK.
Except they don't pay you ANY MONEY.)

Before you get a job,
you need to decide what you want to be
when you grow up.

You could be a Cowboy
or an Explorer
or someone who drives a Big Red Car.
Or even a Super-Ballerina-Soccer-Mermaid-Fairy Princess.
(Like me.)

Or actually ANYTHING you want!

Except you shouldn't be a Robber.
It's not allowed.

(Some people want to be
a Penguin when they grow up.
But that's just silly.)

A good job to get is something you love.
For instance, if you like going on tiptoes best
you could be a ballerina.

Or if you like balls best, you could be a Soccer Player.
Or if you love holding your breath,
you could be a Scuba Diver.

But it must be something you're GOOD at or no one will
want you to do it for them.

Like, it's not suitable to be a World-Famous Chef if you can't even cook cereal.

Or a Hairdresser if you don't know ANY good Hairstyles.

Or a Spy if you don't know any good hiding places and you just sit there and everyone can see you.

If you are a Magician
first you have to find someone you can cut in half
who won't mind.

Then you call them "My Lovely Assistant"
and do Friendly Smiling at them
so they won't run away.

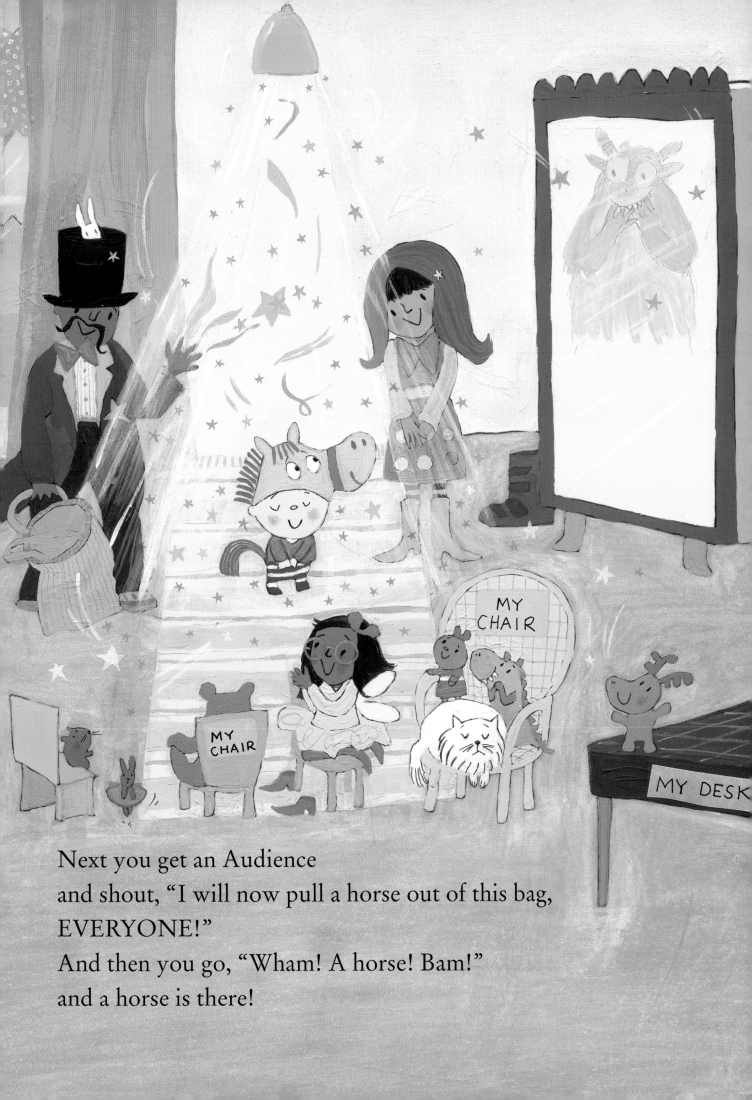

Next you get an Audience
and shout, "I will now pull a horse out of this bag,
EVERYONE!"
And then you go, "Wham! A horse! Bam!"
and a horse is there!

If you are a Doctor,
you need to get a White Coat
and some Patients.

Next you go around with a big needle
saying things like "I'm afraid it's
GANGRENE-CHICKEN-SCARLET-MUMPY-POX!"
and "We should operate IMMEDIATELY!"
and "AMPUTATE!" (which means CUT IT OFF!).

And that's your Diagnosis
(which is what's wrong, basically).

Then you write a Prescription
(which is how to get better)
like "The only cure is M&M's!"

And then you put Band-Aids on
and they feel better.

SCHOOL→

If you are a Teacher,
first you need to find some kids
and make them all come to your School
and Behave.
(Which means not talk unless you say so.)

And they are your Students.

Teachers MUST know all the answers
and how to be NOT BORING.

When your Students are sitting down,
you say, "Listen up! I'm the Teacher!
And I know EVERYTHING!"
Then you give them Projects
and teach them how to learn.

HERE'S WHAT ELSE
YOU GIVE THEM:
• Hard homework
★ Stars (I have ZILLIONS!)
• Time-outs
✓ Laws and Bathroom
Procedures (like "Use
your listening ears!",
"Sit up straight!" and
"Toilet Paper goes IN
the toilet!")

THE BATHROOM

MY CHAIR

If you are a Mommy or a Daddy
first you get some children.

(If you don't have any,
you can practice on your dolls,
or your cat,
or your baby brother.)

Then you put them in strollers
and push them around.

You MUST be good at changing diapers
and not throw up.

HERE'S WHAT ELSE YOU MUST BE GOOD AT:

- Talking to Teachers
- Liking your children more than other people like them
- Protecting your children from hot food, sunburn and Other Dangers
- Tying shoelaces

There are LOADS of other interesting jobs.
Like you could be a Police Officer
and arrest everyone.
Or you could be a Judge
and bang a hammer and go around
deciding things.

You could be a Waitress
and be Friendly and carry food on a tray.

You could be someone who helps people.
Like you could be a Vet
and help a bird.

You could be VERY smart
and know all about EVERYTHING
and write a book called
How to Know EVERYTHING,
by Me, the Genius.

If you practice EVERY day
and get VERY good at reading out loud
you could one day
maybe
become a Babysitter.

When you have chosen your Perfect Job,
you need to Get Hired.

First, you must write down EVERY SINGLE THING
you're good at on ONE PIECE OF PAPER
that's called your Résumé.

My Résumé

I am

good

at

every

(Sometimes it's SO HARD
to fit everything on only
one page, you just have to
use FIVE.)

single
thing
signed
The Boss,
Me

And then you have to keep showing it
to everyone.
"Look, Everyone!" you say.
"See how ABSOLUTELY marvelous I am?"

You must always bring your Résumé when you are trying to get the job.

HERE'S WHAT YOU SHOULDN'T BRING:
- [ ] Your whole family
- [ ] Your gerbils

My Résumé

My Résumé

WHEN YOU GET THERE YOU MUST:

- Knock on the door

- Walk in

- Say your name (so they know it's you) and "How Do you Do" (which is office language and means "Hello," basically)

- Shake hands

- Sit down in a chair

Now you have a "Job Interview."
Which is when The Boss asks you TONS of questions
to find stuff out.
Like, are you a Criminal, for example.

HERE'S WHAT ELSE THE BOSS MIGHT ASK YOU:

- Can you read and write?
- Do you know how to use scissors?
- Can you dress yourself?
- What time is it?

You shouldn't EVER bite the
Boss when he is talking to you.
Or sit in his lap.
Or fall asleep.

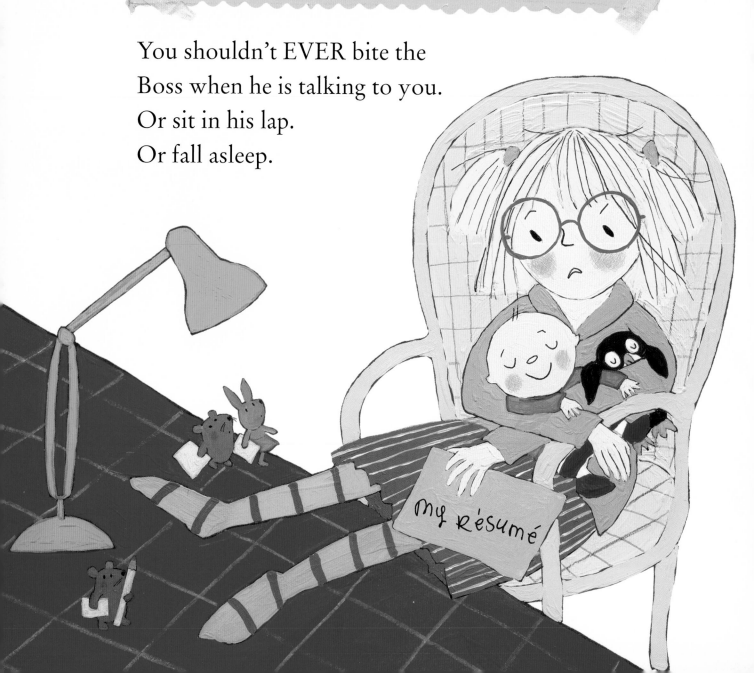

my résumé

You must ALWAYS be on Your Best Behavior.
(Except if you're getting a job as a Horrible Monster,
and then you HAVE to be HORRIBLE.)

At the end of the Interview you say,
"Please may I have the job?"
And The Boss says, "OK, here it is."

And that's when you shake hands again.
And shout, "Hooray for ME! I got the job!
I'm so COMPLETELY GREAT!"

And that's how you get a Job.

Now, basically, you say things like
"I'll take care of it!"
and "Sorry, I can't play Dollies tomorrow,
I have a JOB!"

And after a LONG TIME
if you're VERY good at the job,
and you work REALLY hard,
and you don't bite anyone,
you could actually
become The Boss.
(Like me.)

Sleep Expert

Moose Decorator

Masters of Disguise

Hairdresser

Boot Explorers

Dinosaur Artist

Butterfly Keeper